Dad and Matilda are so happy to see each other.
They agree that the treasure is the most beautiful sight
they've ever seen. They stay for a while but soon
it's time to go home.

"Shall we take a short-cut?" says Matilda.
"A short-cut?" says Dad. "I'm not very
good at those. I think we should
follow your map."

It's true that Dad and
Matilda don't always
see eye to eye...

But they always have
fun together.

There's more to discover in these other titles by Lizzy Stewart:

There's a Tiger in the Garden

ISBN: 978-1-84780-807-3

When Grandma says she's seen a tiger in the garden, Nora doesn't believe her. She's too old to play Grandma's silly games! Everyone knows that tigers live in jungles, not gardens...

This beautiful picture book about the power of imagination is the winner of the Waterstones Children's Book Prize 2017, Illustrated Books Category.

Juniper Jupiter

ISBN: 978-1-78603-701-5

Juniper Jupiter is a real-life superhero. It's no big deal. But something is missing – what is any superhero without a side-kick?

This is a fun and feisty story about friendship and learning to value what you already have.